JEASY CAP
Capucilli, Alyssa
Biscuit wants to play
/
511636

D0010038

MY FIRST
I Can Read Book®

Biscuit
Wants to Play

story by ALYSSA SATIN CAPUCILLI
pictures by PAT SCHORIES

HarperCollins*Publishers*

HarperCollins®, ☙®, and I Can Read Book®
are trademarks of HarperCollins Publishers Inc.

Biscuit Wants to Play
Text copyright © 2001 by Alyssa Satin Capucilli
Illustrations copyright © 2001 by Pat Schories
Printed in the U.S.A. All rights reserved.
www.harperchildrens.com
Library of Congress Cataloging-in-Publication Data
Capucilli, Alyssa.
    Biscuit wants to play / story by Alyssa Satin Capucilli ; pictures by Pat Schories.
        p.   cm. — (My first I can read book)
    Summary: The puppy Biscuit makes friends with two kittens.
    ISBN 0-06-028069-7 — ISBN 0-06-028070-0 (lib. bdg.)
    [1. Dogs—Fiction.   2. Cats—Fiction.   3. Play—Fiction.   4. Animals—Infancy—
Fiction.]   I. Schories Pat, ill.   II. Title.   III. Series.
PZ7.C179 Bit   2001   00-27154
[E]—dc21

                            1   2   3   4   5   6   7   8   9   10
                                            ❖
                                    First Edition

For Peter, Laura, and Billy
with love
—A.S.C.

Woof, woof!

What's in the basket,

Biscuit?

Meow.

It's Daisy!

Meow. Meow.

Daisy has two kittens.

Woof, woof!
Biscuit wants to play
with the kittens.

Meow. Meow.

The kittens want to play

with a leaf.

Woof, woof!

Biscuit wants to play, too.

Woof!

Biscuit sees his ball.

Meow. Meow.

The kittens see a cricket.

Woof, woof!

Biscuit wants to play, too!

Meow. Meow.

The kittens see a butterfly.

Meow. Meow.

The kittens run.

The kittens jump.

Meow! Meow!
The kittens are stuck
in the tree!

Woof!
Biscuit sees
the kittens.

Woof, woof, woof!

Biscuit can help the kittens!

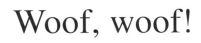

Woof, woof!

Biscuit wants to play
with the kittens.

Meow! Meow!
The kittens want to play
with Biscuit, too!

OKANAGAN REGIONAL LIBRARY
3 3132 01819 5406